MOOMINTROLL
Sets Sail

This book belongs to:

....

Dear Reader,

The book that you hold in your hands is going to whisk you away on an amazing adventure with Moomintroll, his family and their friends in Moominvalley. This story is based on books and cartoons written and illustrated by my aunt Tove Jansson starting 75 years ago – stories that your parents and their parents might even have read!

As a child I used to love listening to stories read aloud by grown-ups. What a wonderful feeling it was to sit curled up in the crook of someone's arm, listening to the story, looking at the pictures, and seeing new pictures drawn in my mind. It was my favourite part of the day, and it made me the book lover that I still am. I hope that these books will inspire the same feeling in you – we're off on an adventure to the magical world of Moominvalley, where absolutely anything can happen!

Sophia Jansson,
Tove Jansson's niece and Creative Director of Moomin Characters

Tove Jansson and some of the inhabitants of Moominvalley.

MOOMINTROLL
Sets Sail

Adapted from the *Tove Jansson* classic

ALEX HARIDI • CECILIA DAVIDSSON • FILIPPA WIDLUND

MACMILLAN CHILDREN'S BOOKS

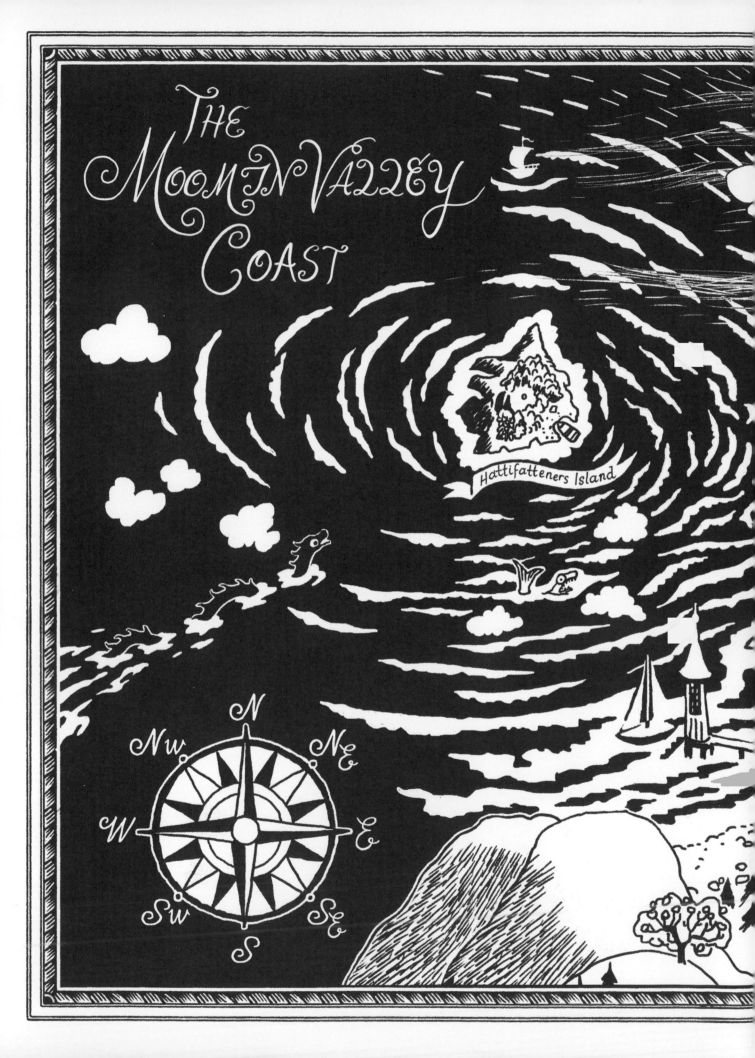

Some of Moominvalley's inhabitants

Moomintroll is curious and friendly. He loves going on adventures, especially if it means spending time with his friends. If ever the adventure becomes too scary, he always has his Moominmamma to come back to.

Moominpappa is a very well-travelled fellow, at least according to him. He often longs for wild adventures like the ones he experienced in his youth. Then he sits in his room and writes his memoirs, a long book about his great escapades.

Moominmamma is soft in all the right places and has a handbag full of dry woolly socks, stomach powder and sweeties. She never loses her cool, and makes sure that every little creature in Moominvalley has a place to sleep if they need it.

Sniff is very easily frightened and a little conceited, but has a kind heart. He dreams of owning valuable things, like gold and jewels . . . or maybe a little kitten of his very own.

Little My is very little, as her name suggests. In fact she is so little that she can hide in Moominmamma's work basket. Little My knows no fear, and when confronted by danger she reacts in the same way as she does when confronted by people in general: by biting.

One sunny, eager morning, Moomintroll, Little My and Sniff went down to the edge of the forest to meet Moominpappa. They were terribly excited and curious, because Moominpappa had something important to show them. He had told them to make sure they were very well prepared, so Sniff had packed all his treasures in his rucksack, just to be on the safe side.

"Welcome, children!" Moominpappa said grandly. "As you may have noticed, I've been rather busy lately. I've been busy building something, to be exact, and finally it is ready. After all, every family has to leave habit and comfort behind sometimes . . ."

"Yes!" interrupted Little My. "We're going on an adventure!"

As they followed Moominpappa through the forest they could definitely sense that adventure was getting nearer and nearer. Eventually they came to a glade.

And there was the boat! It was broad and sturdy,
like Moominpappa himself, and just as fantastic and
fanciful. Moominpappa had called the boat *Ocean
Orchestra*, although he wasn't quite sure how to spell
such tricky words.

Next to the boat stood Moominmamma. She was
tired from loading up the boat, and was trying her
best to get into the adventurer frame of mind

"If everyone's ready, let's get going," said
Moominpappa. But there was one problem: the boat
was on land. It was too heavy to drag to the river.

"If we can't bring the boat to the river, we'll just
have to bring the river to the boat," Moominpappa
decided. "Come on, children!"

They continued deeper into the forest. Moominpappa explained that they were on their way to see Edward the Booble. It was Saturday, and the Booble always bathed in the sea on Saturdays.

"We have to persuade him to bathe in the river instead, to make it overflow," said Moominpappa.

"Is his bottom really that big?" asked Moomintroll.

"Bigger," answered Moominpappa.

"Is he dangerous, this Booble?" Sniff peeped anxiously.

"Well, he steps on people sometimes, but never on purpose," Moominpappa replied. "And he cries for a whole week afterwards. And he pays for the funeral."

"Not much comfort if you're already flat as a pancake," observed Sniff.

"Stay back now," said Moominpappa. And he called to the Booble:

"Hello up there! Where are you planning on bathing today, sir?"

"In the sea as usual, you little sand-flea!" the Booble replied.

"Why not bathe in the river instead? It's lovely and sandy at the bottom."

"Lies! Any toffle knows the river is full of rocks!"

"No, sand!" called Moominpappa.

The Booble muttered to himself for a moment. Finally he said:

"Very well. I will bathe in your stupid river. Now get out of my way. I can't afford any more funerals."

"Run to the boat!" Moominpappa whispered to the others.

And they all ran. They had never run so fast.

Suddenly a loud roar followed by a terrible crash made them all tremble. A tidal wave came rushing towards them. Edward the Booble had sat his sensitive bottom down on the sharp rocks.

The family jumped aboard *Ocean Orchestra* in the nick of time, just as it shot off through the forest.

Off at last! Everybody was delighted, except Sniff. During their hasty getaway his rucksack had opened and his beautiful butterfly brooch and golden sugar tongs had flown out.

"I hope we never have to see Edward the Booble again," said Moomintroll. "Do you think he's terribly angry with us, Pappa?"

"Rather," answered Moominpappa, his paws moving quickly to steer the boat through the trees.

Eventually the boat took one final leap into the river. Then it splashed merrily along and out to sea.

The friendly green forest soon disappeared. Suddenly everything was big and unfamiliar, and strange animals roamed and roared along the steep banks. Late in the evening they came to a deep, solitary bay.

"Cast anchor!" called Moominpappa.

"Right away!" cried Sniff, throwing a large saucepan into the water.

"Was that our lunch?" asked Moomintroll.

"I'm afraid so!" said Sniff. "Sorry about that. It's easy to make a mistake in a hurry."

"Shush!" interrupted Little My. "I heard something."

Everybody pricked up their ears. Then a terrible scream cut through the quiet evening.

"That sounded like a hemulen! We must save them!" cried Moomintroll.

Moominpappa threw the anchor into the water. Then he jumped in after it.

"Never fear!" he called to the hapless screamer. "A moomin is coming!"

Moominpappa swam with all his might as it got darker and darker all around him.

"Get in the saucepan!" he shouted.

Whoever they had rescued was very, very heavy.

"My hero!" Moominmamma said to her husband once they had worked together to get the drenched hemulen on deck. "You've rescued Hemulen's aunt."

"Hemulen's aunt?" cried Moominpappa. He looked bitterly disappointed.

"Shall we throw her back again?" whispered Little My.

Hemulen's aunt was so cross that she totally forgot to thank Moominpappa for saving her life. She had managed to fall in the water while washing her rugs, and now the rugs were lying at the bottom of the sea.

"Give me a cloth!" she ordered. "This place needs a good clean."

"I beg your pardon?" said Moominmamma, her face turning red. "I've just cleaned!"

The next morning they were all woken up
at six o'clock by Hemulen's aunt, who was in
a horrendously good mood.

"Good morning! Good morning! Good morning!
How lucky you are to have rescued me. There's going
to be order around here from now on! Today we're
having a sock-darning contest. Then educational games
as a reward. But first, a proper wholesome breakfast!
No coffee, only porridge."

Hemulen's aunt disappeared below deck to make porridge. Moomintroll, Sniff and Little My seized their chance to hide under the sun tent in the stern. They sat there feeling sorry for each other. They all desperately wanted some coffee.

After a little while they were joined by Moominpappa. Hemulen's aunt had thrown his beloved pipe overboard and he was very cross with her.

Soon Moominmamma crept in too. She couldn't take it any more either, especially since the aunt had started complaining that Moomintroll was badly brought up.

"She can take her umbrella and get lost!" said Moominmamma.

Just then they heard a very odd noise.

It was a muffled sucking sound that seemed like it was coming from inside a metal pipe. It sounded menacing.

Moominpappa peeked out and cried:

"Niblings!"

Moominpappa had met niblings on his adventures during his stormy youth. He explained to the others that they were sociable creatures that lived below the seabed, where they dug tunnels with their sharp teeth.

"They have suckers on their feet and leave sticky footprints behind them. They tend to be friendly but they can't resist chewing and gnawing on anything they get their paws on. Unfortunately they have a fondness for chewing on noses they think are too big . . ."

Moominpappa was interrupted by a loud yelp from Hemulen's aunt.

"What is the meaning of this? What are these things? I refuse to have them here."

"Don't frighten them! They'll get angry," Moominpappa shouted from the sun tent.

"I'm the angry one! Shoo, shoo, shoo!"

And Hemulen's aunt went to smack the nearest nibling in the head.

All the niblings turned immediately to look at Hemulen's aunt. They were clearly eyeing up her impressive nose. Once they were done looking, everything happened very quickly. Niblings swarmed over the rail. The aunt lost her balance and was carried away, waving her umbrella all the while. She toppled over the railing with a scream and the whole company tumbled towards some unknown fate.

Then all was calm.

The family stood by the rail for a long time looking for Hemulen's aunt and the niblings. *Ocean Orchestra* glided carefree across the sun-glittering water as if nothing had happened.

"Niblings are actually pretty friendly," said Moominpappa, much to everyone's relief.

Soon life on board returned to normal. The family scrubbed the deck, which had got all sticky from the niblings' sucker-feet, and drank lots and lots of delicious strong black coffee.

Moomintroll lay on the deck and rested after all the cleaning. The boat rocked gently beneath him. Above him, little white clouds had been thrown into the sky like licks of whipped cream or frolicking woolly lambs. How lovely they were! Suddenly he caught sight of something black flying towards them. Moomintroll sat up.

"Oh look!" he called to the others. "A wolf cloud chasing a little lamb cloud!"

"We have to save it!" cried Sniff.

"I'll deal with this," said Moominpappa. He took out a
long rope and made a loop at one end. Then he tossed it
into the air and skilfully lassoed the cloud.

They all helped to haul in the cloud. It was wonderfully
soft and they hugged it and played with it all afternoon.
As the day went on, *Ocean Orchestra* wound its way round
hundreds and hundreds of little islands. Somewhere
beyond the final island was the blue adventuresome sea.

Evening was approaching, and Moominpappa took out
his nautical chart to find a good spot to stop for the
night. But he made an unfortunate discovery: someone
had gnawed a big hole in it.

"By my tail! We had better moor up before we get
lost," Moominpappa said. "Little My, cast anchor."

The anchor sank to the bottom followed by a rope
stump. Someone had gnawed off the anchor rope.
Someone with very sharp teeth.

"Now we're really in trouble," said Little My gleefully.

Moomintroll looked towards the horizon. He couldn't
see any more islands, only dark, endless waters.

"Mamma, where are we?" asked Moomintroll anxiously.

"We're out in the open sea now, my child," said Moominmamma.

Sniff hugged his rucksack and howled:

"We should never have left Moominvalley! Then I would still have all my treasures. And we would never have come across Edward the Booble and those sticky-pawed creatures. And we would never have got lost . . ."

Just then they heard a gentle cough. One little nibling was still there, all alone under the sun tent, blinking into the darkness.

"Oh," said Moominpappa.

"I'm teething," the little nibling explained timidly. "I simply must bite on something!"

"Little friend, what do you think your mother will say when she realises you've run away?" asked Moominmamma.

"She'll probably cry," said the nibling.

They all forgot about the nibling for a little while as they watched the sunset. It was no ordinary sunset. The sky was yellow, but not a nice yellow. It looked murky and spooky. Ominous black clouds were rising from the horizon.

Moominpappa knew at once that this was serious.

"A storm is coming! We have to go! Quick, all sails up!" he ordered.

But the sails were full of holes.

"Sorry," said the blushing nibling.

Moomintroll felt his snout go stiff with fear.

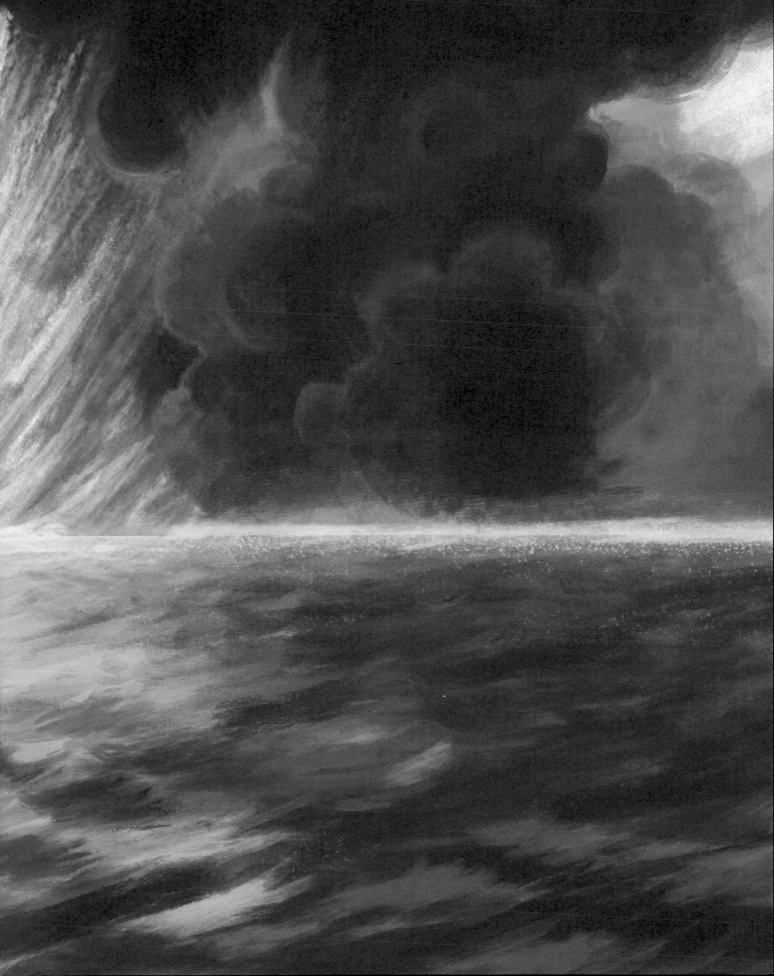

Then the storm came, all of a sudden, like real storms always do. The sun was gone. The horizon was gone. Everything was different and strange. The waves frothed in unimaginable chaos. Everybody was frozen to the spot and held their breath in fear.

Moomintroll thought: *Maybe if I shut my eyes and pretend I'm sitting on the verandah of the Moominhouse on a sunny morning, this will all be over . . .*

After a while Moomintroll could feel that something had changed. When he finally dared open his eyes he was faced with an incredible sight.

Ocean Orchestra was rocking high up in the sky, driven forward by a huge white sail. The storm raged far below them with rolling black waves. It looked like a tiny little toy storm.

"We're flying, we're flying!" cried Little My.

And indeed they were. The cloud they had saved from the nasty wolf cloud had climbed up the mast and spread out like a sail.

"Hurrah!" they all cried in unison.

Ocean Orchestra sailed through the storm. This was a real adventure!

The storm calmed down and the sky began to lighten. Moomintroll shook his paws and examined his tail and ears. No harm done.

"My dears," said Moominpappa. "We've ridden out the storm! We survived!"

But *Ocean Orchestra* was a sorry sight. The mast was cracked and the deck was covered in debris and half-dead little fish.

"Land ahoy!" cried Moomintroll.

Ocean Orchestra sailed straight towards a large lonely island in the middle of the sea. It was strangely shaped, with something that looked like a lighthouse in the middle. And, oddly enough, the lighthouse appeared to be moving.

"Finally something is happening again!" cried Little My in delight.

"Personally I've had enough of things happening," said Sniff.

Ocean Orchestra sailed close to the island. Everybody on board gathered by the railing. Then they heard a rumbling voice coming from high above:

"Ha! Got you at last!"

It was Edward the Booble, and he was in a very bad mood. Would they all be flattened like pancakes now?

In that decisive moment Moomintroll had an idea.
He bravely approached the furious Booble and said in a
calm voice:

"Hello, sir! A pleasure to see you again. Still suffering
pain in the backside?"

"How dare you ask me such a thing, you cheeky
sand-flea? Yes, it still hurts! And it's your fault!"

"In which case we have something that might help.
A booble cushion! Perfect for boobles who have sat on
something hard."

And he sent the cloud up to Edward.

"I know you're tricking me again, you grokefied dish
brushes," said Edward. But he caught the cloud and
sniffed it.

"Hmpf," he said. "I'll just rest for a minute while I
think about what I'm going to do with you . . ."

It wasn't long before the Booble had fallen asleep.
He always did that when he was thinking.

Soon a pleasant wind came and blew *Ocean Orchestra*
away from Edward the Booble and out to sea.

Ocean Orchestra continued its lost, lonely voyage, without anchor, mast or sail. Day after day bobbed calmly by, sunny and sleepy and blue. Moomintroll and the others had long since grown tired of looking for exciting new clouds or strange fish in the water.

One evening at dusk a mail boat came sailing straight towards them. The postmaster waved a letter and announced rather formally:

"This has travelled a long way through storms and lulls."

Moominpappa opened the envelope and read:

I cannot thank you enough for introducing me to the wonderful niblings. We are having a rolicking good time together. We play educational games all day and are looking forward to a wholesome winter with plenty of hearty frolics in the snow.

With gratitude and affection,
Hemulen's aunt

P.S. Please send back the nibling we left behind, his mother won't stop crying.

Moominmamma tied an address label around the nibling's tail and gave his snout a quick polish.

"Now don't ruin the mailboat," she said.

"No no," the nibling promised happily. "Goodbye!"

The night moved in over the sea and everything around *Ocean Orchestra* turned black. Then the night passed and the sun came and coloured the sky with a rosy glow. And on that curious morning Moominpappa stood at the helm as usual, on the lookout for new adventures. Eventually he caught sight of something.

"Come, children! A new adventure is in sight!" he called.

"What is it, Pappa, what is it?" asked Moomintroll.

"See for yourself," said Moominpappa and handed him the telescope.

Moominvalley!

Everyone agreed that was where they should go.
Home. The best adventure of all.

First published 2020 by Bonnier Carlsen Bokförlag, Stockholm
This edition published 2021 by Macmillan Children's Books
an imprint of Pan Macmillan
The Smithson, 6 Briset Street, London, EC1M 5NR
EU representative: Macmillan Publishers Ireland Limited,
Mallard Lodge, Lansdowne Village, Dublin 4
Associated companies throughout the world
www.panmacmillan.com

ISBN: 978-1-5290-4839-1

© Moomin Characters ™
Written by Alex Haridi and Ceilia Davidsson
Illustrated by Filippa Widlund
Translated by A. A. Prime

Illustration on page 4 by Tove Jansson
Illustrations on pages 2-3 and 37-39 by Cecilia Heikkilä

1 3 5 7 9 8 6 4 2

A CIP catalogue record for this book is available from the British Library.

Printed in China